THE SHAPESHIFTER DRIVES A BARGAIN

A COZY ROMANTIC FANTASY NOVELLA

TALES FROM KARNEESIA
BOOK THREE

CLAIRE TRELLA HILL

This one's for Marie,
because of the Rumplestiltskin influence
And also for Anne,
because of Damien Silverleaf being my first "cuddly" love interest

CHAPTER

ONE

T ansy let the cottage door slam shut behind her as she left, basket swinging from her arm, cutting off the last dregs of the early morning breakfast chaos. She breathed a deep sigh of relief.

Once she was out of sight, she tucked her skirts up in her belt, leaving her lower legs bare, and followed the path that led to the swamp. Once she neared the beginning of the cypress and mangrove trees and the saw palmetto and black ironwood bushes, she hung her shoes around her neck, stuffed her stockings in her pocket, and waded in between the cattails and ferns in the streams that fed the waters.

Breathing in the scent of wet earth and life, she went about her business, picking plants to dry, including her namesake, tansy. She carefully dug up a few that looked as if they would survive a transplant to her garden and slipped a sprig or two of wild mint in her mouth to chew on as she journeyed on.

There were so many plants that were useful—for food or for curing different ailments—and even a few that were poison if used wrongly, like nightshade. Part of her healer and herbalist training had been to learn the uses of the plants from old Erna, one of the few residents of her village that wasn't afraid of the swamp. There were creatures to be wary of, true, but that was the same with all wild things, and if she kept a wide berth around them, they left her alone for the most part.

Tansy loved to watch the wading birds stride peaceably through the water, sending ripples out in slow circles. She relished the quiet, even though blue jay and wren cries did not make it precisely *silent*. But no one called her name here, unlike at home with at least three siblings tugging at her skirts and begging for attention or food or tracking mud across the floors, her mother tired and moody, her father begrudging her old maid status while taking most of her earnings as healer and herb wife.

Tansy was rather plain of face, with the same middling brown hair and skin as everyone else in their village, lying so close to the Cadruissau border as it did. She stood short and amply curved, a fact that made her father pinched-faced. Either he wondered why she hadn't caught the eye of one of the village boys and left his house (ha), or he watched the portions she took at supper. Tansy snorted. She took no more than anyone else— less, sometimes. Her body was highly practical and stored up any iota of extra reserves against hard times, just like the squirrels and other creatures did. Sensible of it, really. There'd been enough bad times in recent memory—wars and armed conflicts and the like—that folk were never quite certain if they'd stored enough for winter, if a field would be marched over and salted and their livelihoods ruined, or their cattle stolen by pillaging armies.

And as to courting, it was not as though Tansy didn't want a home and family of her own—beast's teeth, some days she fairly prayed for escape from the riotous nature of their cottage—she just didn't have the patience for the flirting games that some played. She didn't understand it.

And now, having put it off for several years, many girls her age were married and producing their own brood, and the pool of men was dwindling. To top it off, she had garnered the reputation of "odd." But she didn't have to have a man. She'd be perfectly content in a cottage on her own, just her and a hearth and perhaps a cat to keep the mice at bay.

But that was, at best, a fantasy, and Tansy knew it. *Maybe* one day, when she became a full-fledged healer, she might be able to support herself. But she also knew that her father regarded her earnings as family funds. In his eyes, if she wasn't leaving his house to get married (and bringing him a bride price), he would have her earnings since he was feeding and clothing her.

Tansy sighed and swiped a tendril of limp brown hair from her neck. The swamp was just more restful all around.

As she gathered her harvest, she felt her thoughts settle, coalescing into the quiet murmur and flow of the swamp. She worked off muscle memory, letting her feet carry her down familiar paths and stop by recognizable landmarks. As the day waned, she put a hand on the small of her back and stretched, working out the kinks in her muscles. Her stomach growled, another living thing making its demands known, just like the cuckoo's raucous cries. She sighed and lifted her eyes, preparing to turn for home.

But after a few dozen paces, she stopped, unsettled. She was no longer on the faint path she always followed. Tansy looked around at the great stands of cypress, soldier wood, and yellow heart trees, and found nothing that looked familiar.

She had somehow lost the path and found herself in twilight, as fog thickened, with no idea which way led home.

At first, Tansy just retraced her steps, looking for the patches she had just foraged from, attempting to connect her path by stops. That seemed to work for a while, but after a few minutes she felt as if she was going in circles.

"Well, drat," she muttered, planting a hand on her hip. "I suppose I didn't watch where I walked as closely as I could have."

The swamp had a bad reputation among her village, but she

had never felt afraid here before. Not until now, with dark closing in.

If she *had* to weather the night in the swamp, she could. She had gathered wild mushrooms and greens that she could eat, and she could climb a tree, if she felt threatened on the ground.

Possibly, she amended, squinting up at the tall cypress, live oak, and palms that made up the hardwood canopy. Her legs were short.

She turned and blinked as spots of light appeared in her vision. She thought them a phantasm, fading vestiges of the sun under her eyelids. But they did not fade as she squeezed her eyes shut and opened them again. The lights danced in the shadows under the trees.

"Wisps," she said, making a face. Wisps were thought to be many things—faefolk lures, the spirits of the dead, omens of impending doom. "Bother."

Well, there was no help for it. Either she stayed here lost in the dark, the recipient of some dire omen, or walked on towards the dancing spook lights to see what would happen. As the sun dipped low, extinguishing nearly all light, Tansy wiggled her bare toes in the rapidly cooling earth. She was in for a chilly night.

"Well, come on, feet," she said, hefting her basket over her arm.

Picking her way through the swamp took some time. She was careful not to step into a quicksand bog and to test her footing as she followed the tiny dancing lights. The wisps were larger than fireflies and did not move with the pattern of bugs. They never outpaced her—they seemed to be mindful of her speed and were courteous to stay within sight. Slowly, lazily, the wisps moved over the land as the last vestiges of daylight passed away and the world became truly black. The ephemera drifted over the swamp, leading her ever onward.

When they had gone far enough that she felt chilled, her feet ached, and her hands were tired of slapping branches out of her way, palms torn from her labors, the wisps moved together and molded into one large pillar of light amid the dark swamp.

Tansy paused, staring at the pillar of ghost fire as water oozed over her ankles. Blinking, she cleared the spots from her vision just as a man emerged from a tree.

A mangrove dripping with grey moss that waved from its boughs in ghostly strands split open, parting its gnarled bark. A man stepped out of the opening. He stood on one of the root protuberances above the water, his long hair trailing past his knees. It was hard to tell in the washed-out light of the wisps, but it looked red, like blood. His skin was pale, but his eyes burned like black coals.

Tansy took one aborted step backward and froze. Where could she go? Run headlong through the swamp and take a tree branch to the forehead? Fall in a pit of quicksand and drown? Better to present a good front and find out why the wisps had led her here.

At the very least, he may be able to show her the way out.

The man stared at her silently.

Tansy frowned. She wasn't much to look at, but he didn't have to look at her like he'd found something disagreeable under his boot. She had an unremarkable round face with normal brown hair plaited back. Some—*most*—of those strands were escaping, of course, because she had left off her wimple. It was too cloying in the swamp.

Tansy cleared her throat. "I beg your pardon," she said. "I got lost." She lifted her basket. "I followed the wisps because I did not want to stay in the dark. I hope I am not intruding."

The man tilted his head to the side. "After years of sending out my lures, they bring me *you*?"

Me? She swallowed. She did not like the word *lure*.

"Beggars cannot be choosers, I suppose," he said finally.

"I don't want to intrude," she said again, taking a step backwards. "If you could point me back to the path...."

"Hold," he commanded in a hard voice. "I will not start again after years of waiting."

To her astonishment, she found that she could not stir another step. Tansy twisted, attempting to lift her feet, but they were stuck fast in the muck and mire.

The man stepped forward, stout boots protecting his feet from the swamp water, until he came abreast of her. She flinched back and nearly overbalanced when he lifted his hand, but he grasped hold of her chin and peered intently into her face. The wisp pillar helpfully flared, illuminating the intricacies of his angular, sharply-boned face and the severe points of his ears.

Faefolk, some part of her mind gibbered. *Faefolk.*

Well of course, the dry, practical part of her muttered. *He walked out of a* tree. *What did you expect?*

"What do you think you're doing?" she demanded, trying to keep a hold on the panic mounting within her. "What are you talking about?"

"Fishing," he said flatly. "And after years of waiting, I finally have a bite on the line."

"Well, throw me back," Tansy exclaimed. "You can't just—*take* me. I'll be missed. My family—"

"Who?" he said, black eyes sparking.

"My parents. My siblings. They'll worry. I'm the eldest—they need me."

"But no husband," he said. "No child."

She smacked his hand away. Did she have "spinster" labeled on her forehead? "None of your business."

An expression passed over his face too quick to read. "Come inside," he said. "It is cold and wet. Dry yourself by the fire."

"I want to go."

"We will talk about it," he said.

"But my feet are stuck."

"You can move forward." He smiled thinly. "Just not back."

Tansy tried it. She could move her foot forward, but it was as he said. It would not move back. She ground her teeth together, glancing over her shoulder, feeling her choices dwindle. "Please," she forced through numb lips.

"Come into my house."

She shook her head.

He frowned. "Does it matter so very much where we bargain?"

"It does if there is no guarantee I can leave," she said shakily.

"There are no guarantees in life." He reached for the hand fisted in her skirts. "As you like. We will bargain here." His hand was smooth and cool, with long fingers, but there was a deceptive strength in it. She swallowed. He held her scraped hand in his loosely, both of their palms turned upward.

"I will lead you home in the morn safe and sound, if you give me what I ask."

"What's that?" she asked with numb lips.

"Your firstborn child."

Reflexively she jerked her hand, but he held it fast.

"What?" she squeaked.

"I want your firstborn child."

"And if I say *no*?"

He stared at her with flat eyes, but she could very well understand his meaning.

"I won't get out of the swamp alive, you mean."

"If you choose to strike out on your own, it is no business of mine what befalls you. No, I simply will not let you leave."

She pressed her lips together. "This isn't a choice; you're holding me hostage."

"Call it what you like," he said smoothly.

She frantically wracked her brain for a loophole. "What if I agree, and then never marry? Is the bargain null and void if I never have a firstborn to begin with?"

"Oh, you will," he said confidently. "Because if you agree, your firstborn child will be mine."

TWO

Tansy opened her eyes and stared into a highly sardonic gaze. "What happened?"

"You fainted."

It all rushed back—the swamp, the wisps, the faefolk man who parted a tree trunk and emerged, like something out of her nightmares. The shocking thing he had said. The way the blood had rushed out of her head and the whole world had gone black.

He stared down at her, mouth quirking up in faintly mocking twist.

"Beasts' teeth." Tansy squeezed her eyes shut again. She had fainted! Swooned, like some sheltered maiden. She *never* fainted. She was not a delicate wisp. "I was hoping this was a dream." She opened one eye. No, he was still there.

He sat back and rolled his eyes.

She pushed herself up to her elbows and looked around. "Where am I?"

She lay on a plush divan near a crackling fire in a well-lit, cozy room. A soft red blanket had been pulled over her, and her shoes lay by the fire. In the center of the room stood a round table, and low bookcases circled the walls.

"When you fainted, I picked you up and carried you inside."

She stared. Her feet were clean of mud, and her palms sported bandages on the worst scrapes. What had he done that for? "Where's my basket?"

"There on the floor," he said flatly. "You're concerned about the *basket*?"

"It's mine, isn't it?" She craned her neck until she spotted it, and then sat up fully, looking around. "Are we in the tree?" she said curiously.

"Yes. More or less."

"Is it more, or less?"

"Are you concerned about my home, or would you rather discuss the more pressing matter?"

She blanched, remembering what had caused her faint. She clutched the blanket to her chest. Then she dropped it, feeling annoyed and ridiculous.

"I'm not going to ravish you," he said. But the look on his face didn't make her feel secure. He eyed her like a fox might eye a hen far from the henhouse.

She swallowed. Then swallowed again. "No. Just keep me here until I agree to...." She waved her hand.

"Exactly."

She shivered. "It's not a choice."

"It's not designed to be one." He stood and walked to the table, where a steaming teapot waited. He poured the tea into the cups and brought them back, handing her the amber liquid. She stared into the teacup with wary trepidation. Some people said if you ate or drank of faefolk food you never came home again or wasted away for wanting it all the rest of your days.

Her stomach growled, long and loud. Tansy made a face.

"It is not poisoned." He took a sip from his own cup to prove it, challengingly. "Or drugged."

She stared hard into his eyes, trying to see if he spoke truth. Tansy blinked. His eyes were not black, as she had thought, but the deepest, darkest green she had ever seen. She shivered.

I've got to drink something, she thought, *to keep up my strength.*

And—I may be here for some time. Plus—without food, she might swoon again. That was not to be borne. She took a sip from the delicate cup. The tea was surprisingly fragrant and rich. She took another sip to rally her flagging spirits before meeting his eyes. "Why do you want my firstborn child?"

"Why does one usually want a child?"

She glared at him over the rim of the cup. "Why don't you tell me."

"Faefolk in general are experiencing a birth rate crisis," he said, mouth twisting. "In my area, faefolk have not been able to produce any children at all for nearly fifty years. I need my race and line to continue. Mating with a human greatly increases the possibility of fertility and the child surviving to term."

She gulped the tea in her teacup. "Why me?"

"No other human has entered my realm since I began my quest."

"Bother," she muttered, staring into her empty cup. He took it upon himself to fill it. She sipped from the cup, from lack of anything else to do. "So I'm a broodmare."

He looked vaguely affronted. "No, you're the mother of my child."

"Not yet I'm not. Right now, I'm a prisoner."

"Guest."

"Forcibly contained guest."

"However you like." He toyed with the handle of his teacup with his long fingers.

"So you get a whole baby out of this deal, and I get…what? To live? And carry a child for nine months?" *And give that child up?* She had never pictured having a child only to hand it to another, never to see it again. She knew that many fates befell infants— sickness or womb death or difficult births were all realities she was all too aware of as an apprentice herbalist. But to hold a child under her heart for so long…how could she not come to care for it?

The affronted expression returned. "I would provide for you, of course, during your lying-in time, and ease your labor. All your needs would be met."

Her eyes rounded. "You mean you'd be there when the baby was born?"

"Yes," he said testily. "It is my child."

"My child too," she muttered into her teacup. "And all for the very low price of not dying in the swamp, wonderful."

"What would you have me do?" he said harshly. "Walk into your human village and proffer flowers to all the maids there, hoping they do not shriek and scream at my appearance? I will not suffer such humiliation."

Wait, what's wrong with your appearance? she wondered. He was objectively the most handsome man she'd ever laid eyes o—oh. *Oh.* He meant at his appearance *before them all.* His arrival in a human village. A faefolk man showing up. Not….

She worked hard to control her expression.

He continued, "Humans already think faefolk are devils or spirits to make away with their souls. Should I meekly endure being warned away from all eligible maidens, or worse, suffer attacks on my person?" He clenched his fist. "No. I will not do it. The bargain I offer is fair and worthwhile."

Tansy snorted. "Hardly! You get a baby out of it; I get shame and ostracism for the rest of my life. What do you think will happen when I come out of the swamp with—what, a bag of fairy gold? And after, when I start showing. And when you show up to take the child away, *then* what? I'll be ruined forever, and my family will suffer shunning. I don't see how I can accept." *Beyond the whole kidnapping aspect.*

He watched her with his unfathomable green eyes for a long time before saying, "It grows late. Do you wish to continue to argue, or would you like to rest?"

She considered this. "Rest alone?"

"I have said that I will not ravish you," he said firmly.

And I trust your word? she thought, but didn't say it. "If supper comes along with it." She got to her feet and blinked up at him. "What is your name, anyway?"

"I am called Aistin. What is yours?"

"I'm Tansy."

His face went blank.

"What?" she said defensively.

"You…do not look like a Tansy."

"And how do Tansies look?" she said, planting her hands on her hips as she stared up at him. He was far too tall. "Thin wispy wildflowers of girls? Fair of face, dewy-eyed?" All the things she was not, essentially.

He said, "You are far too fierce to be a Tansy," and then blinked, like his words surprised him.

"Oh," she said, somewhat mollified. "Well, that's…fine." Her stomach growled again, and she lifted an eyebrow. "So. Supper?"

THREE

Tansy woke in the soft bed knowing exactly where she was.

After eating a supper of rolls, cold ham, and soft cheese, assembled from she knew not where, the faefolk man—Aistin—had led her from the tree's main room down a twisting stair. At the base was a circular room with five doors in various shades of wood. Glass sconces placed in between the doors glowed faintly. He opened the red door—mahogany?—and gestured. "This room will be yours."

"Where do you sleep?" she had said.

He pointed across the room to the dark door made from what looked like black walnut. "That door is mine. Good night."

Inside her room there was a key in the lock, and she had turned it. Then she had fallen into bed in an exhausted stupor without bothering to undress.

Now Tansy sat up and looked around the room. It was not large. The bed was situated against the wall in a cozy alcove. A soft red rug covered the stone-lined floor, and autumn wall hangings decorated the stone walls. She wondered how the swamp water was kept out.

She threw back the covers and investigated the garderobe,

which was small but serviceable, and did her business and washed. Back in the main room, she tried to smooth the creases from her kirtle, but they stubbornly remained. A clothes press was set against the far wall, but she did not want to root through it. Wearing clothes not her own would be…conceding, somehow. Admitting she would be here for longer than the morning.

She shoved the thought away and unlocked the door.

The atrium was illuminated better than the night before—more lamps were lit against the walls. The circular stair beckoned. Maybe there would be a way to leave if he was not awake yet.

Plus, she was hungry.

With that thought, Tansy applied her feet to the stair, realizing as she did that her shoes were still in the room from the night before.

The main room appeared much the same—the low divan, the fireplace, the table and its chairs, a small bookcase she hadn't noticed before—and the faefolk man sitting at the table with an open book in front of him, sipping from his teacup.

His loose red hair trailed over his shoulders and puddled on the floor beside his chair. He lifted his head, making the tresses ripple. "Good morning." His green eyes blinked. "Are you hungry?"

The adage about eating faefolk food flooded back to her, but that ship had already sailed. "Yes."

He stood and gestured to the seat beside him. He moved to the sideboard and lifted the tray with a covered lid, setting it before her. Under the lid was a steaming breakfast of eggs, bacon, toast, and fruit.

"Did you make this?"

"No." He resumed his seat.

"So there's someone else in this…tree?"

"No."

She considered this as she tucked into the food on her plate, which was incredibly delicious—doubly so since she didn't have to make it. "There are no windows in here."

He quirked an eyebrow at her over his teacup. "Of course not. It's a tree."

"Trees have holes."

"Not healthy ones. Besides, I prefer to not share my domicile with every bit of fauna and flora the swamp can provide."

"So why do you want me here?" she muttered.

He looked up, and his eyes burned into her. "That is entirely different."

"Because I'm a means to an end."

Something flickered in his face.

"Who do you think you are, keeping me captive in order to have your child?" she said, standing.

He stood and glared down at her. "I am Aistin, Nightstalker, Water Walker, of a long and noble line, and I will ensure that line continues, in whatever way I can."

"Have you considered a *compromise?*" She asked acidly.

"Why should I compromise with humans?" he sneered. "It was humans who feared us, always, who stole our magic, who stunted us thus. *You* stole from us; this is my just recompense! I am taking my due."

"At *my* expense!"

He crowded her, pushing her towards the wall, looming down at her, promising wrath. "Believe me, I don't like it any more than you," he snarled.

"I *highly* doubt that!" she yelled. "If I'm such a revolting prospect, throw me back and try again."

"*I do not find you revolting,*" he growled.

The air crackled with tension. Her heart thumped in her throat as she stared up at him, falling into the incredible dark green of his eyes. Tansy swallowed thickly.

He seemed to realize how close they stood, how their heaving chests were close enough to brush given one deep breath. He lifted a hand to her face, brushing her hair from her cheek.

She realized she had never re-braided her hair. It must look like an absolute rat's nest. She ducked under his arm and backed away. Tansy forced through her teeth, "You gave your word." Her body was tingling all over from just that one touch.

He had the nerve to look affronted. "I didn't realize touching a maiden's cheek counted as ravishment. I stand corrected."

Abruptly she realized that noticing the sinuous way he moved, like a liquid predator, his hair trailing across the floor and the lush green of his eyes, meant *she* didn't find *him* revolting either.

Blast, she thought, gulping.

Tansy licked her lips. "Let's think about this logically." She opened her hands placatingly. "Say I have a baby and give it to you. What are you going to do with it?" She waved her hand at the room. "Who's going to change the diapers? What if it has colic? Who's going to provide the milk?"

He paused, considering questions he obviously had not planned for.

Just like a man, she thought huffily.

"Wouldn't it make better sense to find someone who would be willing to bear a child, raise it…be a true *mother*?"

His face closed into a hard mask. "So I must woo a maid without inciting the wrath of her people, bring her home to the swamp, a hostile, dangerous environment where she must stay for her own protection, and bear and raise my child based merely upon my smile and charm?" He snorted, a bitter edge in his eyes. "And you believe any of your fair maids would stay? I have never had any illusions about that. It is a child I am after, not true love. It does not exist, not for ones such as I."

"What do you mean, dangerous?" Tansy asked. "I've never met anything dangerous in the swamp. Unless you mean snakes. And little patches of quicksand. But if you watch your footing—"

"I have enemies," Aistin said. "Those that would work against me. And I am…my magic does not have a pleasing expression."

"What else can you do besides hold me in place?" Tansy asked, fixed between wariness and fascination.

He just looked at her.

"All right, I suppose that's not so important." She twisted her hands together. "I just—don't think I could ever give up my child. That's what it comes down to, for me." She met his eyes. "I don't know that I could feel a child under my heart for nine months and not love it, no matter what it was."

She turned away, but not before she caught the much-struck look on his face.

AISTIN HAD DISAPPEARED. Where, Tansy wasn't sure. But she could find no door that led out of the tree. Possibly it took magic to open the passage. *Why am I not surprised?* She also could find no door that led to kitchens or any kind of preparation area. Only the stair down to the five doors below.

Tansy curled up on the divan and watched the fire pop, idly wishing that she had learned to read more than the bare minimum required for her herbalist apprenticeship. She wondered what all those books contained. It *was* rather nice not to have any chores, to have meals that she did not have to prepare and no constant litany of demands to satisfy. She could hear herself think. But now she was left with what to do with herself. She picked up the book Aistin had been reading and flipped through the pages. It was hand-written—possibly a journal? But she couldn't read script.

With a sigh, she put the book down and investigated the book-shelf. Most were weighty tomes she couldn't begin to pick through, but there was one slim volume bound in soft leather. She pulled it free from the shelf. It opened to a beautiful watercolor of the swamp in early summer. The light glinted off the delicately rendered dogwood trees and white wild indigo, the variety of green and yellow shades gleaming off the paper. She turned the page to find another watercolor—this one of a heron poised to take flight, so vivid it might have been about to leap off the page.

Tansy moved back to the divan and slowly turned the pages. The whole book was full of pictures, swamp flora and fauna, with a few lines of text under each that she could read a few words of. The images were fantastically beautiful. She had never thought her wild and rough swamp could be so lovingly rendered.

"My mother made that book."

Tansy jumped and hastily grabbed the book before it fell off her knees. She looked up at Aistin, who watched her with an indecipherable look as he stood in the stairway.

"She painted it?" Tansy asked. "It's beautiful—so lifelike."

"She painted all the watercolors and wrote the descriptions." He sat in the chair next to the divan.

Tansy stared down at the text, where only a few words—woodrat, summer, stick—made sense to her. "I can't read much of it," Tansy finally admitted. "I can't read much besides plant names, numbers. Things like that."

"May I?" He held out his hand for the book.

Tansy reluctantly handed the book to him.

Aistin inspected the page she had been looking at—a picture of a woodrat, its long tail and large ears and eyes lovingly rendered. "This says, 'Woodrats are very fond of shiny objects. One quirk of the woodrat is that if you offer an item they want, they will drop what they are carrying to "trade" for the new object. They also build nests out of sticks that are handed down from generation to generation.'"

Her eyes widened. "Our generations or woodrat generations?"

"Both, perhaps, depending on how long the woodrat line has survived." He raised a brow. "My mother wrote the book as a nature and wildlife manual, to document everything in our domain, but she compiled it when I was a child. That's why she took such care with the pictures. She wanted to make sure I understood and loved our duty of care."

"It's lovely," Tansy said. "A wonderful gift."

"She died before I matured," Aistin said with no emotion. "A hunter's arrow."

"Oh," she whispered. How awful. But what a precious treasure to have from her hands.

"My father faded to a shade. He remained until I came into my full power and could take on the mantle of caretaker from him, but after that he gave himself to the swamp."

She stared at him with huge eyes. "That's *horrible*."

"He missed her," Aistin said simply.

"Well, so did you!" she exclaimed. "But he just *left* you? Alone?"

"I was grown."

"*So?*" she said in outrage. "If *I* was your mother, I would've had some *words* for him!"

A tiny smile flashed across his face as he looked up at her. "This page is one of my favorites," he said, flipping to the heron in flight.

"I saw that one," she said. "It's fantastic. It looks as if the heron is going to leap into the room at any moment."

"This is what it says," he said, and began to read.

As she watched him, Tansy thought, *He's so alone. And for how long? Faefolk are said to be long-lived. The solitude…it must be crushing. But he wants to consign a child to the same fate?*

She swallowed hard against the sympathy taking root in her heart.

Tansy spent three days in the tree, sometimes with Aistin, sometimes alone as he went she knew not where to do she knew not what. Sometimes they argued—her demanding he let her go, he insisting she agree to the terms of his bargain. She knew she would be missed, and her family—well, at least *some* of her family would worry for her. But it didn't seem to hold as much urgency here in this tree abode.

More and more Tansy found, to her guilty discomfort, that she was enjoying herself as they sat in companionable silence or spoke amicably about the swamp or her herbalist apprenticeship, or as Aistin read aloud from some of his books to her as she knitted.

She had insisted on something to do if she was to be cooped up, and he had finally provided her with yarn and needles. She wasn't quite sure *what* she was knitting, but she casted on a great number of stitches, so whatever it was, it was big.

The evening of the third day—or what she assumed was evening, because they were eating the third meal of the day, Aistin set his spoon down and looked across the small table at her for a long moment. "Would you consider a compromise," he finally said, apropos of nothing. "I would allow you to visit the child."

Tansy blinked, her spoon halfway to her mouth. "Oh, *now* we're compromising?"

"Take it or not."

She dropped the spoon back in the soup bowl with a clink. She crossed her arms. "Oh no, now we're *negotiating*. What if *I* keep the child, and *you* visit it."

He pursed his lips, an expression far too recalcitrant to be attractive. "The child must be raised as my heir within my demesne. It must receive regular tutoring and training. Also, I cannot leave my land for too long unattended."

She frowned. "Wait, before you said you'd attend the birth."

"That is a necessary trip to ensure your survival. Regular trips leaving my land would invite predators eager to wrest it from me."

Tansy licked her lips. "You're aware we're discussing this like we've made a decision? But I haven't even agreed to any of this yet."

He blinked slowly, staring at her with a hunter's eyes. Deep pools of green that she was liable to drown in. "I'm patient. I can wait."

"But I don't like you. Or even respect you. How do you have a child with someone you don't know?"

"The land gives me a greater Knowing to those within my borders. That's how I knew you were there and brought you to me. And we have had these days." He raised an eyebrow at her. "Your kind makes marriages based on land and coin. What 'knowing' exists there?"

Grasping at straws—why did it feel like time was somehow spiraling out of her hands?—she said, "What if I want more time to know *you*?"

His expression darkened. "You don't want to know me." He stood abruptly from the table, a strange, wild look crossing his face before disappearing. "Tonight is a hunter's moon. I can feel it in the air. Be sure to lock your door."

Tansy didn't bother to say that she always locked her door here. "What is a hunter's moon?"

"It's a time when blood feeds the swamp."

FOUR

She didn't lock her door.

What Tansy did do was wait by her door, listening. She had to listen hard because his butter-soft leather boots made almost no sound when he walked, but his hair still swished along the floor, even braided, and she heard the telltale hiss in the night. She wasn't sure how late it was, but he probably expected her to be asleep.

Tansy waited until she heard him ascend the stair, the soft susurrus fading.

And then she opened her door and followed.

She wore good boots she had found in the wardrobe and a pair of breeches and tunic in soft green wool. Surprisingly, they all fit her. Her cloak was thick and warm, but knee length; it wouldn't soak up any water and become weighty. Her hair was braided back out of her face. She could do this.

Her boots were not as quiet on the steps, which was why she had to lag so far behind. But she was tired of his obfuscations, his avoidances, his outright refusal to answer her questions. She'd learn what a hunter's moon meant to him…and maybe why he was so insistent that no human woman would want him willingly.

The door now…that presented a problem. She had given the matter some thought over the past few nights. Tansy didn't know how the spell worked, or why she could never find the door when it was shut, but she *could* see it when it was open. And it opened and shut slowly.

So, yes. Her plan *was* "follow him out the door as fast as possible and hope he didn't see her do it."

She poked her head up the top of the stair, just in time to see his cape flit through the open doorway. She hurried forward as silently as she could as the door began to twist closed, the bark unwinding, the entrance sealing itself from top to bottom.

Tansy thrust herself forward through the diminishing opening, feeling the bark scrape her sides, catch at her cloak, tugging, holding—

She jerked herself through as the passageway snapped closed. She rested, panting, against the tree, before scanning the area. Well, Aistin wasn't standing there glaring at her, so that was something.

She turned to look at the tree. A scrap of cloth from the bottom of her cloak fluttered, caught in the otherwise seamless tree trunk.

"Uh oh," she muttered. He would know…but she mentally shook her head. He was always going to know she was out. It was inevitable. This was about something else—about asserting her personhood. He couldn't just bottle her up.

As Tansy carefully picked her way through the swamp, watching for his tracks, the thought crossed her mind that she could go home, in theory. If he wasn't aware of her departure, he couldn't actively confuse her path…unless that Knowing he spoke of alerted him….

She blew a strand of hair from her eyes. She had many questions about faefolk magic. But regardless of whether she could get out of the swamp, he had warned her he could find her. And she did not want to bring wrath down on her village or her family. They wouldn't know how to handle him.

Tansy followed his tracks for a while, and then realized she could see his silhouette in the darkness through a stand of trees.

She froze. He wasn't doing anything, just standing there. Had he seen her?

She ducked down and crouched behind a cypress tree, watching the sight. The moon touched his hair like liquid silver, washing over him like water. He lifted his face to the moon, his eyes closed.

He stood like that for some time, bathing in the silver moonlight, though the moon itself looked red and dark, and then his form shimmered, twisted, molding its shape.

Tansy's eyes widened. She pressed a hand to her mouth.

Aistin bent, his tall body changing. His long braid of hair became a tail, his hands and feet paws. His face changed. Under the moon's glow, the panther shook itself, the powerful muscles rippling underneath the thick fur. Its eyes glowed brightly, surveying its dominion, and padded off through the grove of trees.

She stared after it, struggling to swallow. She managed it on the third try.

Well, that explained all the allusions to his nature.

Tansy slowly straightened, feeling all her bones and muscles protest. Fear wanted her to stay contracted into a small ball, hiding from the predator. With effort, she straightened her shoulders. She didn't care what shape he was in; he was still the same self-absorbed faefolk man. She wouldn't be cowed by him.

Well, clearly the hindbrain part of her cared, but it was overruled. Tansy forced her legs moving and set off in pursuit again.

She had vague thoughts of staying downwind, to keep her scent from being detected, but she couldn't feel what direction the wind was blowing from. She had never gone hunting; that was thought to be the male purview. Foolish now. She could have used some of that knowledge.

Tansy followed him for some time. At first, she thought the panther was just wandering around in the swamp, but after a while she realized he was traveling in a specific path. Walking the boundaries, she thought, though she couldn't say where the thought had come from.

The panther's long, thick tail swept back and forth as it padded on velvet paws, stalking through the cypress and the poisonwood trunks, stopping to sniff patches of ground here and there. There was an awkward moment when it stopped to mark a patch of orchids, and she hovered behind a tree until she heard the stream of liquid stop.

She had just climbed over a fallen tree when she stepped wrong. Under her foot a twig snapped, and just like that, the night sounds of wind and insects and the sigh of sleeping creatures stopped. She found herself alone in loud silence.

But not for long. The panther appeared; its large, lonely eyes fixed on her.

Tansy bit her lip. Then she raised her hand tentatively and waved.

The panther's lip curled in a snarl, and its form shimmered. Aistin resumed a more man-shape, but his physique was muscled along the lines of the big cat's, and his face retained the harsh lines of the predator as well as the glowing eyes and fangs.

She blinked, and he was right in front of her, clawed hand gripping her chin.

"What is it that you do, you thorn in my flesh?" he growled in a voice as deep as the night.

"I wanted to know," Tansy said, and swallowed. "I wanted to see."

"Well, now you have seen," he purred, putting his face close to hers. "And what do you think?"

His red hair spilled over his shoulders, but his face was still furred. She lifted a hesitant hand to touch the tresses and then rub his furry cheek. "It's…cuddly?"

He drew back, affronted. *"Cuddly?"* he said in outrage. His eyes burned into her, sending conflicting emotions through her.

On the one hand, scary panther that might eat her. On the other....

"Well," she hedged, shuffling her feet and tugging on an earlobe, uncomfortably reminded of the rosy fantasy of a small cottage and a cat by the fire. *It's sort of similar....*

He tensed, his head shooting up. Extremely elongated ears twitched, swiveling to find the sound.

She froze, hardly daring to breathe. Then she heard it—a faint hiss, the swish of water.

He snarled silently, and she got an up close and personal look at his white, sharp fangs.

"Up the tree," he growled. "*Now.*"

She turned to eye the high fork in the tree trunk behind her. *Short legs*, she thought gloomily—but squeaked when he grasped her around the waist and bodily lifted her into the tree's boughs. She caught the branch above her and swung herself up onto it.

"Keep climbing," he commanded.

"What about you?" she whispered sharply.

But there was no reply.

Her panther-man strode away from her cypress tree into a pool of moonlight. He growled, "I know it's you, Golgrotha. Cease your skulking in the shadows. You trespass on my ground."

From the darkness came a splash, as if something very heavy had heaved itself out of the water. Tansy's heart thumped.

Slowly, slowly, a reptilian form slithered into the moonlight. It paused, mouth open, as if tasting the air.

Aistin did not move.

Then the long maw full of jagged teeth snapped shut, and the alligator blurred, picking itself up off the ground to assume the hulking form of a man, dripping water. He was muscled and covered in the armor of his beast form, but the most unnerving thing about his appearance was his wide mouth, full of sharp teeth, smiling. "Aissssstin, old friend," Golgrotha hissed.

"I am not your friend, and you tread on my land, swim in my waters. Are you eager for a reckoning?"

"The humanssss erode my territory. Steal my game. My prey," Golgrotha said. "Mine. All Mine. They would be easy prey."

"You spend too much time as a beast," Aistin said in a low voice. "You forget what you are."

"I know what I am. Ssstrong. Powerful." The alligator man smiled wider, his teeth gleaming. "Stronger than you." Without warning he lunged forward, reaching for Aistin with arms like tree trunks.

Aistin whipped out of the way, circling Golgrotha, claws extended. He watched for an opening.

Tansy gasped and searched for a stick or something to throw. Something. Anything! But there wasn't. She hurriedly began a descent from the cypress, finding handholds but also slithering down the trunk in order to get to the ground. The alligator man was so much bigger than Aistin. He would need help.

However, when she reached the last branch, Aistin caught sight of her movements and snarled wordlessly, his eyes flaring in alarm. She found herself pinned to the trunk, unable to move. *No!* she screamed silently. Her jaw would not move to let it out.

As she railed against her bonds, Aistin spun on the alligator man and clawed him, digging into the joints where his reptilian plates did not fully cover his skin. Golgrotha snapped his teeth and threw his weight, and the two of them went down to the ground.

They rolled over the ground, battling for dominance, for supremacy, kicking, punching, clawing. Golgrotha did his best to perform a death roll, but the ground was not soggy enough, the water too far to accomplish what natural alligators did by drowning their prey.

Aistin managed to hook his wicked claws into his opponent and rip through muscle down to the bone.

Golgrotha howled and backhanded Aistin away from him. Aistin flew through the air, corkscrewing his body to land on his feet. They met again in a clash of claws and fangs.

Tansy silently chafed against her invisible bonds. Aistin had no natural defenses like Golgrotha, no plates to protect sensitive skin and organs. Much of the blood flying must be coming from him.

Golgrotha tried to grapple Aistin again for a death roll, but Aistin picked up a rock and smashed Golgrotha's skull with it, speaking a string of hard, sharp syllables. There was a harsh burst of light. Golgrotha dropped like a felled tree trunk and lay there, panting and twitching in the leaf matter.

"Take yourself away, enemy mine," Aistin growled, more cat than man. "Slink back to your den where you bide. Remember where my territory lies and remember this day. Remember that you have another nature, and that you lost this fight because you neglected it." He flexed his clawed hands. "Begone."

The word echoed with power, forcing Golgrotha up to his hands and knees when he would have stayed supine in the dirt. Slowly crawling away, his form shifted into that of a full alligator. He slipped into the water and was gone.

Aistin held his dominant pose a minute longer, and then sighed. He sagged to his knees.

The magical hold on Tansy relaxed.

Freed of the confinement, Tansy slithered down the tree trunk and ran forward. Seizing him, she dragged him to his feet. "Are you badly hurt?" she demanded.

He hissed but shook his head. "No. I will heal."

"Good." Tansy slammed her fists into his shoulders, smacking at him with her paltry strength. "Don't you *ever* freeze me in place again! Especially if there's danger! You numbskull, you brainless fool, absolute *lunkhead*, I could have *helped* you!"

He seized her wrists. "Helped me? You think you could have *helped* me? When you put *yourself* in danger, by deliberately disobeying me, sneaking out, and then I had to come to your rescue?"

"What, did you think you were being *noble?* He didn't even notice I was here. Do you have *rocks* for brains—"

His mouth descended on hers.

Now *she* felt like she was under siege. His mouth moved over her lips like a brand, claiming, devouring, pressing into her mouth, taking no prisoners. She moaned against him as he transferred her wrists to one of his hand so he could grasp her around the waist and haul her against him.

"Little termagant," he hissed against her lips.

She mumbled, "Proud, stuck up—"

He stopped her mouth with another sweltering kiss.

She found herself pressed back against the tree, held up by his arms like bands of iron around her as he kissed her until she couldn't remember her own name. He had evidently decided that she was too occupied to keep hitting him, because he had released her hands. She threaded her fingers through his hair, reveling in the long, silky texture. She sunk a hand into the fur around his oversized, rounded ears, and she felt his chest vibrate. *Purring?* She wondered hazily as her other hand wandered over his broad back, pressing him closer to her. Her fingers encountered a warm, tacky substance, and he flinched under her touch.

She pulled back, blinking the kiss haze from her eyes. "You're hurt."

"Not badly." He tried to capture her lips again.

"No, no!" She pushed against his chest. "We have to get you seen to. Clean those cuts! Who knows what that nasty alligator had under his claws?"

"Magic will see to them," he insisted.

"*I'm* going to see to them," she said firmly. "Now."

WHEN THEY REACHED the tree with her swatch of cloak sticking out of it, Aistin gave her an irritated look but said nothing as they stepped inside the tree. Tansy eased him down onto the divan. "Tell me where I can get water and cloth." She still had her basket of herbs, which she had hung up to dry the first day—she could make a salve of some of them if he had nothing readily available.

"Say what you need, then open the cupboard door," he said, growling as she tried to inspect his wounds. "But I will heal."

"Don't you move," she said fiercely, pointing at him, "or I'll thump you."

"Does that work?" he said, raising an eyebrow.

"It does on my younger brothers. It would be close call on who is squirrelier—them or you." She walked to the cupboard where she had seen him get some items during her stay here and shifted her feet. She felt a little silly saying "Hot water, clean cloths, and salve" out loud, but she did it. She pulled open the door and stared in amazement at the steaming bucket of water and jar of ointment, as well as a tea tray piled high.

She stood back from the door and pointed. *"How?"*

He stared at her blank-faced. "Magic."

"Oh, *magic,*" she repeated in a sarcastic voice, pulling the bucket and tray from the cupboard. She set them down with a thump on the table and dunked the cloth in the water, wringing it out. "Skin your shirt off. Or do you need me to cut it off?" She had shears for her yarn around here somewhere.

Aistin gingerly removed his shirt, wincing.

"I suppose it was magic that let you turn from a full panther to a man wearing a shirt and breeches?" she asked. "I noticed that alligator man wasn't wearing anything in the way of clothing."

He shot her a dirty look as he tried to pull his hair free of the shirt.

"Here." She helped slip the red tresses free of the fabric. Heat crept up her neck as she remembered threading her fingers through the strands, his mouth on hers. When she got a look at his broad chest, the heat made its way to her face. *You're a healer,* she told herself sternly. *You have brothers. You have seen the male body unclothed before. This is nothing new.*

When she got a look at the claw marks that scored his back, she sucked her teeth and pressed the cloth to them, cleaning them of the dirt and who-knew-what contamination from alligator claws.

He flinched and hissed at her as she did so.

"Maybe if you had let me help, this wouldn't have happened," she said virtuously, coating on salve.

"And how would you have helped, pray tell?" he demanded. "With no defenses, no magic?"

"I could've thrown rocks to distract him, found a branch to hit him with. Any number of things. Now we'll never know because you decided to be high handed." The cupboard had provided more cloth with which to wrap his wounds, and she wound it around his chest, forcing her hands to be steady and professional.

"So, you don't want me to be noble?" he said, frowning. "I was trying to protect you."

"No! I don't need protecting. I want you to be…what you are."

"And what am I?"

"A frustrating, fatiguing, furry, frank, fascinating…fae," she ended lamely, staring down into his deep green eyes.

His expression turned intent. "Fascinating?"

"Facinorous," she snapped, using a word he had defined for her during one of their reading lessons. "I meant to say facinorous."

"Aye, that's right," he said, standing. "I am very wicked."

She swallowed.

"And furry…." His eyes glowed with the magical light of the panther. "You don't mind that I turn into a beast?"

She shook her head.

He took a step forward. "With claws? And fangs?"

Tansy shrugged, using all her willpower not to take a step back.

"And I'm frustrating to you?" he purred.

"That's right," Tansy croaked, jutting her chin out. "Incredibly frustrating."

"Well, that's too bad," he murmured, and made as if to turn.

A strangled noise erupted from Tansy's throat. She jolted forward, reaching out to him.

And then his arms were around her, his lips on hers.

His lips fanned the embers that had been kindled in the dark swamp, and they burst to life within her. She clutched his shoulders as Aistin lifted her as if she weighed nothing, crushing her to him. She gave in to her longing and buried her fingers in his hair, and he growled against her mouth. "Tansy…."

"Yes," she breathed. "Yes, yes, yes."

FIVE

Tansy stretched luxuriously, enveloped in softness and warmth. She cuddled closer to the most comfortable pillow that rose and fell—

Her eyes flew open.

She saw the bandages she herself had wrapped around a very male chest, the tangle of red hair flung every which way, even over her. She sighed and snuggled closer to Aistin, enjoying the feeling of being small for once. It made sense now—the dual nature of his polished, refined faefolk side melding with the wildness of the panther. She had felt beautiful, cherished. Even perhaps....

Under her head, she felt his chest vibrate with a purr. His muscled arm came around her, holding her close. "I trust that you are frustrated by me no more, madam?" he rumbled in her ear.

"Frustrated, no," she whispered. "Fatigued, yes."

He laughed softly, his hand tracing the curve of her shoulder down her arm. His eyes were bright with mirth. "I suppose I should apologize again to make amends."

"If you like," Tansy said, lips curving up in a smile.

His lips brushed hers softly, once, twice, as his hand caressed her skin. As his fingers trailed over her stomach, he froze. An expression of wonder and wild delight crossed his face. "Tansy, we—"

"What?"

He stilled, looking at her.

"Aistin, what is it?"

A muscle in his jaw worked.

A premonition swept through her. "Tell me."

"We—we have conceived a child. I can tell."

She sat up abruptly as reality came crashing back with a horrible vengeance. "*What?*"

"There is life there," he said stiffly.

"Was this your plan all along?" she demanded without thinking. She clutched the sheet to her chest.

His face closed into a hard, tight mask. "I did not force you or do anything of the kind—"

"Did you magic me?"

As soon as she said the words, she knew it was the exact wrong thing to ask.

"Did I encourage a pregnancy through magical means, you mean?" he said, hoarfrost dripping from the words. "Or did I manipulate you into sharing my bed?"

"That's not what I—"

He stood and paced away from the bed, reaching for a robe thrown over a chair. "I did neither. However, as a healer and herbalist, you know that conception can occur after only one attempt."

Her cheeks heated. "I *know* that, but—"

He spoke over her again. "As per our terms, you are now free to go. The wisps will lead you back home."

"*Fine,*" she shot back. "You got what you wanted. Now you just try and collect," she snarled. She'd like to see him try. She'd never agreed to his stupid bargain! He had *no* hold over her! Conceived, *ha!* How could he know? She was the healer, not him! In nine months, they'd see. She'd show *him.*

She wrapped the sheet around herself and stalked out of his room as he said nothing. Did nothing.

She kicked the door shut.

Then she heard an almighty crash, as if he had thrown something tremendously heavy at the wall.

"*Tansy!*"

The cry echoed over and over from her mother and sisters—and even her little brothers gave her hugs and allowed her to ruffle their hair.

The deep furrow between her father's brows eased as he caught sight of her, relief spreading over his face. Then he bellowed, "Where the great bloody hell have you *been*? It's been four blighted days, you addle-pated girl!"

"I roamed too far and got lost," she finally said, after he had shouted himself hoarse. "I found a cottage to stay at. It took a little time to retrace my steps. I'm fine. Now I know the way and won't go astray again."

She could tell her parents were still suspicious of this story. Her father might've accused her of slipping away to meet a man, but she was sure he had made the rounds in the village and knew very well that she hadn't been with any of them.

But there was no need to tell them the real tale. At best they wouldn't believe her anyway. At worst, someone would get it in their fool head to hunt the "creature of the swamp that carries away young maidens." Though she wasn't young, and maiden… she shoved it from her head to consider later.

She also didn't interrogate why she considered that to be the worst-case scenario.

Tansy had missed home. Even sharing a bed with her sister again was comforting…the first night. After that, she woke to elbows in her side, hot feet on her in the night. Snores. Not to mention the rest of the house's nocturnal noises. And she kept waking in the early light of dawn, hearing the awful words she had thrown in Aistin's face.

Her days reverted to their typical rhythm, too; helping her mother with meals, wiping runny noses, scrubbing mud from the floor, helping diagnose and dose the village aches and pains. But it wasn't enough anymore. Truth be told, it had *never* been enough, and it was just more apparent now.

The morning of her third day home, the moment she had the house to herself—a rare occurrence—she had brewed a cup of tansy tea. She had stared into the teacup for an age until the tea had gone cold and her mother had returned from the market.

Then she had thrown it out.

Tansy didn't even know if Aistin had told her the truth, but... her voice from days ago came back to her: *"I don't know that I could carry a child under my heart for nine months and not love it."*

She knew that nothing was certain. Women miscarried. They thought they were carrying when they weren't. Babies died in the womb, were born stillborn or choked by the cord. And many other perils loomed after birth. But...she clutched the small flicker of possibility to her chest. She could not snuff it out. She wanted that possibility. It was *hers*.

And she wanted it, faefolk father or not. Conditional clause or not.

"We'll see," she promised herself, rolling up her sleeves. *In nine months, come what may, we'll see.*

Let him come. We'll see who gets the last word about this child then.

CHAPTER
SIX

It only took Tansy six weeks to lose her mind.

As summer waned, her siblings needed shoes and warmer cloaks and lost all the aprons and caps she hemmed for them when she could find a moment to breathe in between cooking with her mother and handling the herbalist potions and salves she brewed weekly for the common complaints of cough, colds, stomach complaints, fever, and minor burns. Every payment twisted deeper and deeper as the coin or barter of a few eggs, butter, bread, or what-have-you went to her father's pocket or the family table.

And she loved them, she *did*, but more and more, especially as she became convinced that she was with child, she longed for something that was just hers. A place, a thing…a person.

She also realized raising a baby—or even just revealing that she was pregnant to her family—would be difficult. Immensely so. Her father, a traditional man, would not keep her under his roof. He would insist she marry someone. Anyone, to save her reputation. If not…. Tansy kept swallowing down the early morning nausea as she imagined what would come after. Ousting —to protect the rest of the family from stigma and shunning. It was a small village, and her father needed his salary, small though it was.

This isn't my fault! Tansy thought angrily as she scrubbed clothes in the washtub. Well...some of it might be. A definite portion, in fact. But *most* of it, she thought indignantly, the majority lay with *him*. After all, who had lured whom and basically kidnapped her in the swamp? Not her. So, it was only fair, the *bare minimum*, that he contribute to finding a solution. One that wouldn't wait for nine months to be up.

She'd journey to the swamp again, that's what she'd do, and lay the problem before him and ask, *"What are you going to do about this, oh high and mighty faefolk lord?"*

Tansy nodded decisively, wringing out a sheet. She'd go tomorrow, early, before her nausea had the chance to sink its teeth into her, and she could use the pretext of gathering herbs. She needed more anyway. She had avoided the swamp for a long time, after...well. Everything.

Her heart spasmed. She had missed it.

———

BUT AS IT TURNED OUT, she didn't have to make the journey after all.

Once the sun had dried the freshly scrubbed shifts and sheets and napkins and aprons pinned up on the clotheslines, Tansy went to take them down and fold them before sticky-fingered children dirtied them again. She had just finished unpinning a wide sheet when the cloth fluttered down, revealing another person.

Tansy jumped back in alarm. Her jump unbalanced her, but long fingers clamped around her arms, steadying her. Grounding her.

"Aistin," she said dumbly.

"Tansy."

"What are you doing here?" she demanded. "It hasn't been nine months."

"Tansy, no." He swallowed. "I will not hold you to a bad bargain I never should have made—"

"Well, good, because I never agreed to it in the first place."

He opened his mouth, but before he could speak, her mother came around the side of the cottage, saying, "Tansy, once you've finished here, I need you to—*oh!*" Her sentence ended on a shriek.

"That's torn it," Tansy growled.

As her mother proceeded to have strong hysterics, the cottage quickly emptied of children, crowding around their mother's skirts, peering wide-eyed at the visitor.

"Tansy, who's this?"

"Why's his hair so long?"

"His ears are funny."

"He's so tall!"

"Why's Mama screaming?"

Tansy inspected the faefolk man who had appeared in their cottage garden with new eyes. Red hair in intricate braids falling past his knees, the strange clothes—unusually fine, she noted with a surprised eye—of rich velvet, long fingers that sported rings on every digit and clutched...a huge bouquet of wildflowers? And last the elongated face and ears that marked him as other. *Very other,* she thought, recalling the lithe panther stalking through moonlight.

What her mother marked as frightening started a flutter in Tansy's chest.

After letting them exclaim for a long minute, Aistin swept his commanding gaze over the chattering throng and announced, in ringing tones, "I have come to ask Tansy to be my wife."

Instant silence swept over the group—even silencing her mother mid-yelp, leaving Tansy's flabbergasted, "You have?" all too clear.

His eyes returned to hers—those deep green eyes. "Yes. I came to beg your forgiveness. I was...in no way trying to trick or trap you. I was wrong to try to do so in the first place. And I am here to beg you to come back to me." He elegantly spilled onto his knees, making her rock back on her heels, and held out the bouquet.

The blooms shook, just slightly, in his grasp as he held them out. His long-ago words came back to her: "…*Walk into your human village and proffer flowers to all the maids there…? I will not suffer such humiliation…*"

"Because I do not want to be without you. Not for any other reason," Aistin said with a significant look. He took her free hand twitching in her apron. "But because I spent these last weeks empty, listless, in anguish. I've never been more alone since you left. I saw what could be—and I lost it because of pride and foolishness. Tansy, I miss you. I want you. My existence was empty—*is* empty, and I only realized once you brought warmth and life back to my home. To *me*. And I in no way deserve you. I have much to do to make amends with you. But you are my heart."

How much must it have cost his immense faefolk pride to come and kneel before her, in front of her *family*, no less? He missed her *that much*?

Tansy's throat felt curiously tight.

"But if you do not forgive me, if you tell me to go my way and never return," he said, with a level look that clearly was doing serious work to conceal the anguish within him, "I will. I will leave you in peace. Forever. I promise."

He'd give up the baby. The child he had wanted so much.

Just to make it right.

Because she meant more to him.

It took two tries to make the words come out, but Tansy finally planted her hands on her hips and squeaked, "You sneaky cat, you stole my thunder! I was going to find you in the swamp tomorrow—"

Aistin shoved up off his knees and swept her up into his arms, stopping her mouth. She buried her fingers in his hair and kissed him back.

The cottage door slammed, and she belatedly realized one more player had yet to take the stage.

"What's all this then?!" her father bellowed, taking in the tableau.

Aistin set her down, but Tansy did not let go of his hand. "I have offered for your daughter's hand."

"And I have accepted," Tansy interjected. "I love him. We're going to live in the swamp. I will come back to visit."

"You love me?" Aistin repeated.

"Live in the *swamp*?" her mother exclaimed.

"Yes, the swamp. He's…he's the lord of the swamp. Right?"

Aistin raised an eyebrow. "Well—"

"You'll be a *lady*?" her mother said, eyes opening wide.

"And of course I love you," Tansy told Aistin, ignoring this. "You wouldn't make me so exasperated if I didn't love you."

Her father, not tracking this conversation well, swelled, ready to bellow again from frustration.

But in Aistin's hand there suddenly appeared a large pouch. "Sir, I understand this is a sudden request, to take your daughter from you. But I love her and will care for her as the most precious thing I possess. I know is the custom of your people to exchange a bride price when a daughter leaves home. I humbly ask you to receive this, knowing that it is little recompense for the loss of such a gem."

"Gem?" Tansy asked under her breath.

"Pearl beyond price?" Aistin suggested.

She flushed. "Hardly."

"No," he said, squeezing her hand. "So much more."

Her father hesitantly took the pouch and opened it. Tansy could see the gleam of gold—and the decided clink of coin from the bag. Her father's eyes widened in shock. He looked up at Tansy. "You want this man, Tansy?"

"Yes, Papa," she said, using the childlike name she had left behind several years ago.

"And are set on him, right enough," he said, eyeing their clasped hands. "Stubborn as a mule."

"Who do I get that from?" she said tartly.

The corner of her father's mouth quirked, seemingly against his will. "Have him then, and welcome."

TANSY RUTHLESSLY PACKED up her belongings, as her mother bustled about ineffectually and tried to press on her items for a hasty trousseau as well as dubious tonics for childbearing.

I'm the herbalist, not you, Tansy thought, but said nothing about their dodgy nature. She wouldn't be needing them anyhow. She left the bulk of her herbalist supply for her younger sister, who had shown promise about the identification and preparation of her remedies. Tansy told her to speak to the village herbalist for teaching.

She was able to dodge most of the skirt-pulling from the little ones, as Aistin proved to be the main entertainment draw. He sat on the bench in the garden and entertained the little ones by making a coin appear and disappear in ears and noses and reappear in his fingers. "Not magic," he told his wide-eyed audience. "Sleight of hand." And proceeded to show them how the simplest tricks worked, giving them each a thin copper coin to practice with.

"Thank you for training up the village's next generation of confidence tricksters," Tansy said, dumping her sack of belongings onto the bench.

"I decided it was safer to make sure they knew it was a trick and to show them how to do it so that if anyone ever decided to start rumors of how the faefolk monster came out of the swamp and stole you away with his dark magic, they'd be able to counter such accusations."

"Ahhh," Tansy said in comprehension. "I see. 'Oh, you mean the faefolk man who taught me how to pull coins from your nose? Yes, very scary.'"

"Exactly so," he said tilting his head back so that his eyes caught the light.

"You're always looking three steps ahead."

"More like seven. Because you are precious to me. I swear to you, Tansy, I will put no fetters on you. I was wrong to ever try to do so in the first place."

"Yes, because you try to handle everything yourself," she said wryly, even as her heart swelled. "And....?"

He blinked. "And?"

"I said I loved you," Tansy said patiently, "but—"

Just then the whole of her family came to wave them off, and it was hugs and kisses and sobs and hugs all around, until Tansy forcibly broke free. "I love you all! We are going now! I will be back to visit. Goodbye!"

Aistin shouldered her belongings as Tansy took him by the hand and pulled him down the road towards the swamp, while her family waved them on.

Once they were down the road a way, Aistin said, "Well, that went better than I expected."

"What did you expect?"

"More screaming. Perhaps pitchforks." He wrapped his free arm around her shoulders. "I would've faced a whole village of pitchforks for you, Tansy."

"You would've faced losing what you wanted most," she said quietly.

"Yes," he said, stopping. He took hold of her chin so that she met his eyes. "*You*. I love you, you know."

"I *do* know," she said testily, "because you told my *father* first before you told me—"

"I'm never going to live that down, am I?"

"Not for a while," she informed him.

"Would reminding you that you *also* told your father before telling me help or hurt?"

"See, I told you *right after* that I loved you," she insisted. "You were much tardier."

Aistin laughed. "I'll make it up to you. I promise." He pressed his lips to hers again as they walked down the road towards the swamp.

BONUS EPILOGUE

"Shh, shh, shh," Tansy heard, drifting out of the fog of sleep. "Mama is sleeping. You kept her up all night. You are so stinky. What a stinky kitten. Let's change that nappy."

An unhappy mewl from the nursery was quickly countered by a comforting purr.

Tansy sat up in her and Aistin's bed and stretched. The night before had been a long one, with an unhappy baby just starting the teething process. Usually, Aistin could sooth their child back to sleep with little issue, but he had been out on patrol through the swamp, as problems arose near the full moon. When he had returned, he had taken the unhappy baby from her and sent her off to bed to sleep.

She must've slept for some time; she didn't feel nearly as tired as usual. Tansy gathered up her hair and braided it back before she slipped on her knitted shawl and padded to the nursery. She peeked in the doorway. The nursery was dim, the only light the small glowing crystal on the night table. The intricately carved crib, with all of the swamp's birds hanging over it, was empty, but a large panther lay stretched out on the thick rug. Its eyes glowed, reflecting the light of the crystal. A tiny kitten mewed and attempted to attack her father's thick tail on wobbly legs.

"There's my girl," Tansy murmured. She moved forward and ran her hand over the massive panther's head. A purr rumbled into her hand for a moment before the shape stretched and morphed into her husband, his hair spilling over her hand and down onto the rug. Delighted, the tiny kitten pounced.

"Did she wake you?" Aistin rumbled, his eyes flashing green, the panther still close to the surface.

"No," Tansy said. "Woke up on my own." She crouched down to lean against his shoulder. "You know she's going to want to change forms every time she has a dirty nappy if you keep this up."

"We already have trouble keeping the blasted things on her," he chuckled.

Tansy reached for the kitten and cuddled the soft fur. The baby made a happy noise and became a round-cheeked baby of four months. Tansy smiled into the face of their little Calla, with her shock of bright red hair and her green eyes. The baby made a happy noise at seeing her mother and reached out her tiny hands.

Tansy kissed the baby's hands and then kissed Aistin's cheek. "Was everything all right on your rounds last night? I forgot to ask."

"Yes. Everything is just fine." Aistin curled an arm around them both. "And look—Calla's first tooth came through."

Tansy leaned closer. "Is that what I think it is?" She tried to open Calla's mouth and got a bite for her pains. "Ow." The small, sharp tooth protruding from the gum winked at her as her baby daughter stared at her with wide-eyed outrage.

"Her first eyetooth. She's a cat through and through," Aistin beamed. They had wondered how much of her father's powers Calla would inherit, and here was the proof.

"What am I going to do with two sneaky cats under one roof?" Tansy said, laying her head on his shoulder.

"What indeed?" Aistin said, holding her closer. Tansy felt the rumble in his chest. He was purring.

And the tiny baby she held started purring, too.

ALSO BY CLAIRE TRELLA HILL

Gothic Vampire Romance

Black and Deep Desires

Parfit Gentil Knyght: an Addie and Etienne Vignette (Newsletter Exclusive)

The Karneesia Chronicles

The Erlking's Daughters

Mistress of Wardwood and Other Stories (Newsletter Exclusive)

The Flight of the Spellbound

The Heartwood's Choice

Tales from Karneesia

When a Dragon Comes Courting

Come by Water

The Shapeshifter Drives a Bargain

The Lost Treasures of Peredur

Aeronwy's Stolen Child (Newsletter Exclusive)

ABOUT THE AUTHOR

Claire Trella Hill will read anything, but fantasy romance and gothic fiction are her favorites. Born and raised in Houston, Texas, she still lives there because she is impervious to 100 degree weather. She also has a bad habit of making her characters in the Sims and continuing their stories. When Claire isn't writing, she can be found with her nose glued to her library app, assisting with the last tricky pieces of a puzzle, swilling Dr. Pepper, collecting vintage romance covers, or cuddling with her cat.

You can connect with her on social media or sign up for her newsletter on her website ClaireTrellaHill.com.